CONTENTS

3 IN 1 VOLUME 1

LAST SON OF KRYPTON

THE MUSEUM MONSTERS

TOYS OF TERROR

First published in this format in 2014 by Curious Fox,
an imprint of Capstone Global Library Limited,
7 Pilgrim Street, London, EC4V 6LB
– Registered company number: 6695582

www.curious-fox.com
The moral rights of the proprietor have been asserted.

Art Director: Bob Lentz
Designers: Bob Lentz and Richard Parker
Production Controller: Victoria Fitzgerald
Editor: Dan Nunn
Originated by Capstone Global Library Ltd
Printed and bound in China by RR Donnelley Asia

ISBN 978 1 78202 111 7
18 17 16 15 14
10 9 8 7 6 5 4 3 2 1

A CIP catalogue record for this book is available
from the British Library.

LAST SON
OF
KRYPTON

WRITTEN BY
MICHAEL DAHL

ILLUSTRATED BY
JOHN DELANEY AND
LEE LOUGHRIDGE

SUPERMAN CREATED BY
JERRY SIEGEL AND
JOE SHUSTER

BY SPECIAL
ARRANGEMENT WITH THE
JERRY SIEGEL FAMILY

CHAPTER 1

THE DYING PLANET

"Our world is doomed!" said Jor-El. He faced a group of leaders and scientists on his home planet of Krypton. He spoke with anger, not in fear.

"The fate of this planet, and everyone on it, rests in your hands," Jor-El continued. "Earthquakes have rocked Krypton for many months. Tidal waves have flooded our coastlines. Volcanoes have erupted at the edges of our cities. If we do not act now, everything we have worked for will be destroyed!"

Behind the group of scientists stood a strange, metal figure. The figure, a supercomputer in the shape of a man, stepped forward. His metal head and glowing eyes towered above Jor-El.

"This is nonsense, Jor-El," said the supercomputer. "Krypton has revolved around her red sun for millions of years. Our planet will continue to revolve for a million more. Safely and peacefully."

"Not according to my research," said Jor-El.

"Your research is wrong," said Brainiac calmly. "My brain has been going over your figures for the past several weeks. And the answer I come up with is this: Krypton is simply going through a phase. In a few months, the volcanic activity will stop."

"That's impossible," said Jor-El.

Brainiac's eyes glowed brightly. "Have I ever been wrong before?" he asked.

Jor-El was silent.

"I am not wrong this time, either," said Brainiac.

As the metal man spoke, the crowd nodded. They were calmed by his words.

"With all due respect, there is always a first time for being wrong," warned Jor-El. "The pressure inside our planet is growing. This is *not* simply a phase. This is the entire destruction of our world. We must leave Krypton before it explodes!"

Someone in the chamber cried out in alarm. A murmur of panic passed through the crowd. Brainiac raised his hands.

"Jor-El fills you with fear," Brainiac said. "He controls you by frightening you."

"No!" said Jor-El. "I do not seek power. I only seek the safety of my fellow citizens."

"If you care for their safety, then you will keep silent," said Brainiac. The lights in his metal skull were blinking angrily.

Another figure stood up. It was Vond-a, leader of the science council. She stepped on to the floor and stood between Jor-El and the robot.

"I agree with Brainiac," she said. "Your words will only panic the good people of Krypton, Jor-El. If Brainiac's supercomputer brain tells him that the planet is safe, then it is safe."

Jor-El knew it was useless to argue. He had been warning the scientists for weeks.

The scientists never listened. Now, Jor-El bowed his head. He said, "I will obey the decision of the council." Quietly, he left the chamber.

Brainiac watched Jor-El walk away. Dark thoughts hummed through the supercomputer's brain. *Jor-El is right,* he thought to himself. *Krypton will explode. But these fools must never know.* An evil smile crossed Brainiac's face. *Jor-El must be silenced.*

CHAPTER 2

A SPACESHIP TOO SMALL

Miles away, Jor-El stepped out of his flyer pod. He entered his living chambers. His wife, Lara, greeted him nervously.

"Did the council listen to you, Jor-El?" she asked.

Jor-El shook his head. "They listened to Brainiac instead," he said. "He doesn't understand the danger we're in. Something must be wrong with his programming."

Suddenly, the house shook. Several windows on the floor above them shattered.

"Another earthquake," said Lara.

The shaking stopped as quickly as it began. "I've been tracking quakes all over Krypton," she added. "They're growing stronger. There are more of them. Your calculations are right, Jor-El."

The couple hurried to their lab. "There's no comfort in being right," Jor-El said. "Especially when it means our world will be destroyed."

Jor-El checked his monitors. "I'm afraid it's worse than I thought, Lara," he said. "Krypton's core is heating up. The pressure is growing faster than I predicted."

"What does that mean?" Lara asked.

"Krypton will explode in a matter of days, possibly even hours," he said.

"What about our son?" Lara gasped.

Jor-El nodded. "We must get him at once and bring him to the launch port," he said.

Lara rushed down the stairs to the nursery. Before she entered the room, she smiled. She could hear their infant son cooing happily in his crib.

"Kal-El," she called.

The baby boy turned at the sound of his mother's voice. A wide grin stretched across his face. He held out his arms, wanting to be picked up.

"Oh, Kal-El," whispered Lara. She held the child tightly to her chest. "What a good boy you are."

Lara quickly grabbed some red and blue blankets to wrap the baby in. Then she hurried to the launch port to join her husband.

The port was at the top of their living quarters. A wide, open window showed a view of the entire city.

Lara entered the port. She saw Jor-El working on the model of a transport rocket ship. She hugged the baby even tighter.

"I had hoped that we would have time to build larger transports," said Jor-El. "They could have safely carried our people to another planet. To a new home."

"Now," he added, "this small model can carry only one." Jor-El looked down at his smiling son. The baby wrapped a tiny hand around his father's finger.

Another quake rocked the building. A light fell from the ceiling and crashed at Lara's feet. The baby cried out. "Jor-El, we must hurry," Lara said.

Jor-El checked the control panel for the rocket launcher. Lara placed the baby's blankets inside the ship. She made a warm, inviting nest to hold her son. Then she stared at the boy as he sat on a nearby table. "You have no idea how important you are, do you?" she said. "Kal-El, you are Krypton's last hope."

Another crash echoed throughout the building. Lara quickly scooped up her son.

"That wasn't an earthquake," said Jor-El.

"It came from downstairs," said Lara.

Jor-El switched on a video monitor. The monitor was connected to a camera built into their front door. As soon as the monitor blinked on, Lara grabbed her husband's arm.

Vond-a, the head of the science council, stood outside their living quarters. Standing with her was a squad of security troopers, fully armed.

"Jor-El!" she shouted. "Open the door! Your family is under arrest!"

CHAPTER 3

ESCAPE!

Outside Jor-El's and Lara's living quarters, the troopers were startled by a new noise.

ZWWWOOOOMMMM!

A fiery object flew across the sky.

"Is that a meteor?" asked one of the troopers.

"No meteors were predicted at this time," replied Vond-a. Just then, another tremor rocked the planet. The troopers were thrown off their feet.

Miles above them, the flaming object flew out of Krypton's atmosphere. The council leader was correct. It was not a meteor. It was a spaceship. And inside the ship was the supercomputer Brainiac.

It would be a shame if I stayed behind and was destroyed, thought Brainiac. *My super brain is worth more than a million of those puny Kryptonians.*

He set his ship's controls to take him to a distant galaxy called the Milky Way. "The advanced knowledge of Krypton shall survive in me. With that knowledge, I will conquer another world," he thought.

Brainiac's ship streaked through Krypton's sky. Meanwhile, Jor-El checked the controls of the smaller ship in his launch port.

"It's almost ready," he said to Lara.

His wife was saying goodbye to their infant son. The baby lay inside the ship. He was wrapped in a cocoon of red and blue blankets.

"Be good, Kal-El," she said. Her eyes filled with tears. "You will find a new home, a safe place far away from here."

A loud crash sounded below. The security troopers had knocked down the front door.

Jor-El pressed a remote control. The doors of the small ship closed with a hissing sound. The lock clicked. Then a loud humming filled the room.

As the humming grew louder, the ship lifted into the air. Little Kal-El was unaware of what was happening to him.

Kal-El rested in his soft blankets. He was secure inside the unbreakable walls of his father's creation.

"Don't be afraid," Jor-El said, turning to his wife. "We will always be a part of Kal-El."

Lara gazed at the rising ship. "We will never forget you, my son," she said.

"There they are!" A trooper was standing at the door of the port.

He pointed into the room at Jor-El and Lara. The rest of the squad gathered behind him. They drew weapons and marched into the room.

"Move away from the controls, Jor-El!" commanded Vond-a.

"Don't, Jor-El!" shouted Lara.

"Stay out of this, Lara," said Vond-a. "Your husband is a danger to the planet of Krypton."

"You are the danger to Krypton!" cried Lara. "My husband was only trying to save us. And now he is trying to save –"

"Quiet, Lara," said her husband.

The council leader looked around at Jor-El's scientific equipment. "What is going on here?" she asked. "And what is that ship doing?" She pointed at the object floating high above the floor.

The troopers aimed their blasters at the small craft. "It is obviously some kind of weapon," said Vond-a. "Shoot it down."

"No!" Lara screamed. Jor-El threw himself in front of the troopers.

A bright light filled the room.

THWOOOOMMMMMM!!

The small ship flashed out of the room. It flew with such force that everyone inside the launch room was hurled against the walls. Outside, the ship streaked through the sky. It looked like a shooting star.

Faster and faster, the ship raced above the surface of the planet. It rose above the vast cities. It rushed past the highest clouds. Within seconds, it was speeding past Krypton's three moons.

Gazing into the sky, Jor-El and Lara followed the trail of their vanishing son. They held on to each other. A powerful quake shook the city. The walls were torn away from their building. The rays of the planet's red sun filled the launch room, turning it the colours of blood.

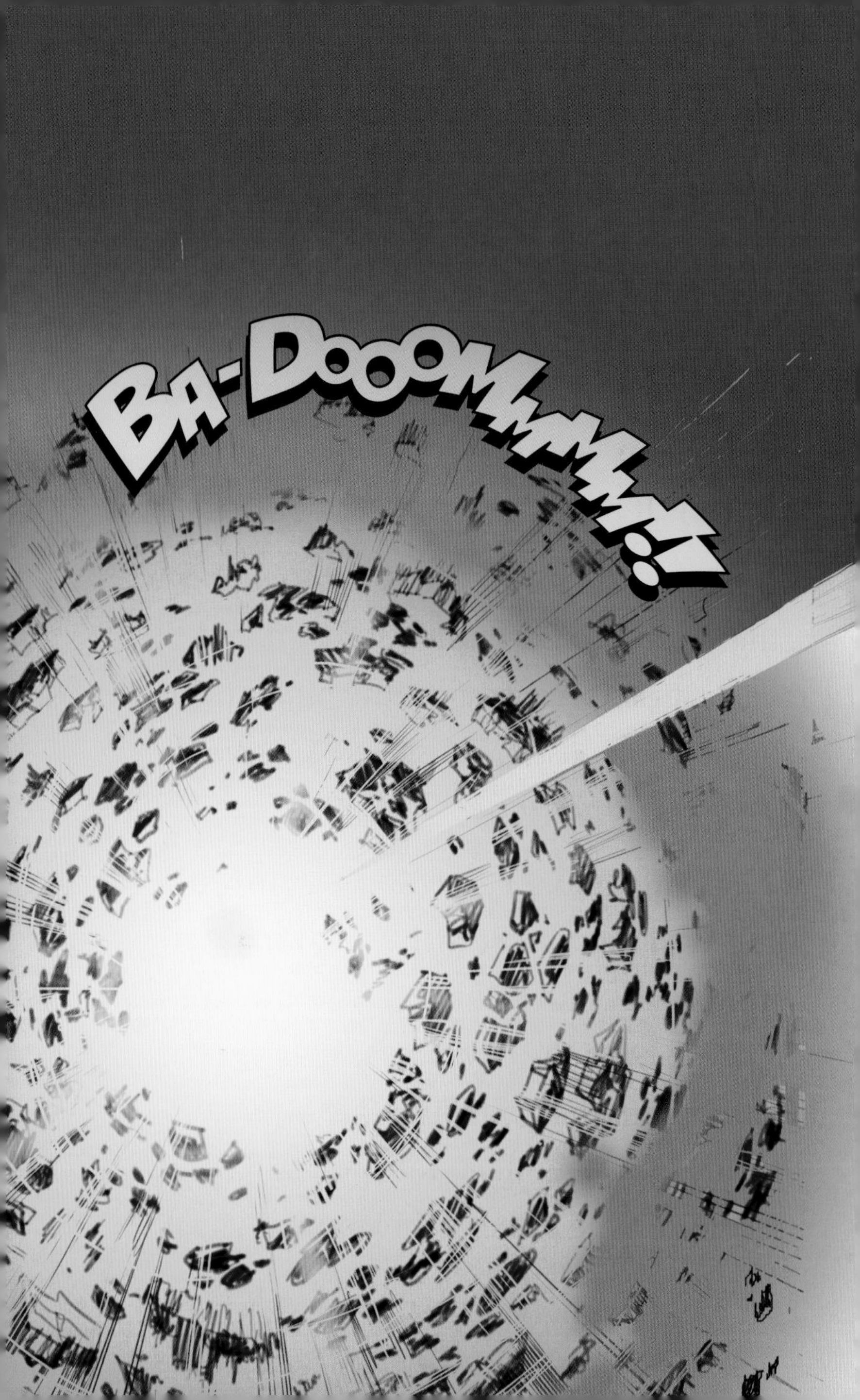
BA-DOOOMMMM!!

"Good-bye, Kal-El," Jor-El whispered.

As Krypton's greatest scientist had predicted, the huge planet exploded. Continents were ripped apart by volcanic force. The oceans evaporated. The sky itself caught on fire. A billion lives were lost in a second. But one small life sailed swiftly away to another planet.

CHAPTER 4

A NEW HOME

It was a summer day in Kansas. A
yellow sun floated in the blue, hazy sky.
The hot sun beat down on the fields around
the town of Smallville.

On a farm outside of town, Jonathan
Kent stared at the rows and rows of corn.
He was sitting in the cab of his combine.
He had been driving up and down the rows
of corn for hours.

He had farmed these fields for many
years. He wondered how many more years
he would be driving this combine.

BZZZT! His mobile phone rang. Jonathan pulled it from his belt. "What is it, Martha?" he said.

"How did you know it was me?" asked his wife on the other end.

"Who else would it be?" Jonathan said with a smile. "You're the only one who ever calls me on this thing."

"You could at least be polite and say hello," said Martha Kent.

"What was that?" yelled Jonathan.

A fiery ball rushed past the cab of the combine. It missed hitting Jonathan by just a few feet.

"Jonathan, are you all right?" yelled Martha's voice from the phone.

"I don't know," he said. "I think I just saw a meteor."

"It's a meteor all right," said Martha. "I can see it from the kitchen window."

The combine was thrown into the air. Jonathan braced himself against the cab's door. Martha screamed. Cows in a nearby meadow tipped over. From the edge of the field, smoke and flames could be seen.

"Whatever it was," Jonathan said to himself, "I think it just landed."

A few minutes later, Martha joined her husband in the field. They walked carefully towards the rising smoke. The meteor had dug a huge crater in the soil.

When they came near the edge of the crater, the Kents stopped.

"Maybe we should call the police," said Martha. "Or a science teacher from the school."

"I don't believe it," said Jonathan.

He took off his glasses and wiped them with a rag. "That doesn't look like a meteor to me," Jonathan added.

"What's it supposed to look like?" asked Martha.

"A rock, Martha. A big ugly rock. But this is smooth and shiny." Jonathan took a step forward. "Oww," he groaned.

"Careful," said his wife. "You were knocked about in that combine."

"I'll be careful," he said.

The object was smooth and shiny, as Jonathan had said. It did not look like a rock from outer space. It looked more like a piece from an aeroplane.

The object wasn't burning. The smoke came from a few cornstalks that had caught fire from the crash. The farmer bent down to get a closer look.

"Don't touch it!" cried Martha.

"Oh, for Pete's sake, Martha," he said. "I just want to –"

"What was that?" cried Martha.

Soon, a hissing sound filled the crater. A metal panel on top of the strange object began to open up. Martha and Jonathan both froze.

Two tiny hands rose up from the opening. A small head covered in dark hair peeked over the edge.

Martha ran down into the crater. "It's a baby!" she said.

"It's a little boy," said Jonathan, stunned.

A toddler looked up at them from the shiny object. A wide grin stretched across his happy face. He held out his arms, wanting to be picked up.

"Where did you come from, little man?" asked Jonathan.

"A baby!" repeated Martha.

"Yes, I can see that, Martha," he said.

"We've always wanted to have a baby of our own," she said.

"He doesn't belong to us," Jonathan pointed out.

Martha reached out and lifted the toddler into her arms. "I don't think his family is from around here," she said. "Unless you see someone else falling from the sky."

"Oh, Martha," said her husband.

Martha Kent stared happily at the little boy. He smiled and grabbed at her hair. "I think we'll call you Clark," she said. "I've always liked that name."

Jonathan shook his head. "We can't do this, Martha," he said.

Martha stuck out her chin. "We're only going to take care of Clark until someone else comes looking for him," she said.

Martha looked up at the sky and then back at her husband. "But somehow I don't think that's going to happen. Do you?" she asked.

Jonathan put his arm around his wife's shoulders. The new family walked away from the crater and headed towards their house.

CHAPTER 5

SUPERPOWERS

Late that night, Jonathan and Martha hitched the strange object to the back of their combine. No one else saw them drag it into their barn. Then Jonathan began to dig a hole in the centre of the barn's dirt floor.

"I don't want any nosy reporters looking for this thing," said Jonathan. "They'd never leave us alone."

Martha agreed. She was also worried that Clark might be taken away from them.

While Jonathan kept digging, Martha carefully searched the inside of the metal ship. She looked for clues about the strange baby. There were no photos, no toys, and no clothes.

"Look at this," Martha cried.

Her hand touched a bundle of red and blue blankets. She pulled them out and examined them closely.

"I wonder if these are from Clark's home," she said.

Once Jonathan buried the ship, they returned to the house. Martha walked upstairs and tucked the blankets deep inside a clothes chest in her bedroom.

"Clark may need these some day," she said to herself.

Over the next few days, Clark was a happy toddler. He enjoyed his new home. He was interested in the cows, the tractor, and the dogs. But most of the time, Clark stayed close by Martha. Something in her tender voice was comforting to him.

When Martha worked in the garden, Clark sat next to her. He dug his fists into the dirt. Martha would brush off a carrot or peapod and hand it to him. Then the boy would hungrily stuff it into his mouth.

That summer in Kansas was one of the hottest on record. Martha worked in the garden in the afternoons, when the sun was behind the big barn.

Clark didn't seem to mind the heat. The little boy didn't sweat. His skin didn't burn. In fact, Clark was happiest when sitting outside in the hot yellow rays of the sun.

ZHH'INNGG!

Clark looked up at the weather vane on top of the house. It was spinning wildly. Martha noticed it too.

"Jonathan," she yelled. "I think we're in for a storm."

Jonathan was fixing some equipment in the barn. He didn't hear his wife's voice.

Martha stood up from the garden. She stretched her back. She was about to grab her buckets of carrots when she stopped.

Off to the south-west, the sky had grown greenish-black. Dangerous clouds drifted towards them. In the middle of the dark clouds, a grey cloud was spinning. It spun like the weather vane. Martha watched as a tongue of twisting air dropped from the sky.

As soon as the twister touched the ground, the tongue changed colour. Now it was dark brown, the colour of the dirt it was scooping up into its deadly funnel.

"Jonathan!" screamed Martha. "A twister! There's a twister!"

The whirling storm was heading towards the farm. Martha reached down and grabbed Clark's arm. She pulled him along behind her. They raced towards the storm shelter at the side of the house.

By the time they reached the shelter, powerful winds began to blow across the fields. The corn was pushed flat to the ground. The trees groaned and creaked. The weather vane suddenly snapped off the roof. It landed nearby on the ground, nearly hitting Martha and Clark.

Martha screamed again for her husband. She pulled open one of the storm shelter doors. It was low on the ground. Short wooden steps led down to a shelter built under the house.

"Jonathan!" she yelled again. "Where is your father?" Martha cried to Clark.

The little boy stared up at her face, puzzled. He could tell she was frightened. Things were falling around her, scaring her.

Clark was reminded of something that had happened far away. He didn't like it when people were afraid.

Finally, Martha saw Jonathan step out of the barn. "Here!" she yelled, waving her arms. "We're back here."

Jonathan ran towards her.

The sound of moaning metal grew louder than the storm.

Jonathan stopped and turned. He glanced at the silo that stood between the barn and the house.

The metal tower was rocking slowly back and forth. It began to pull away from its cement floor.

Another, louder, groan filled the air.

Jonathan was frozen with surprise as he watched the silo fall on to the ground.

Then he started running again. "Hurry! Hurry!" Martha yelled to him.

She turned to Clark, to push him into the storm shelter. The boy was gone.

Martha looked up at Jonathan. She wanted to yell at him, but the winds were too loud. He would not hear her saying that Clark was missing.

Then she saw him. Clark had wandered around the side of the house. He stood directly in the path of the rolling silo. In a moment, the metal tower would crush him.

Martha started to run after him. She knew she was too far away to reach him in time. There was nothing else she could do. Suddenly, the silo was on top of Clark.

The boy raised his little hands. His tiny fingers reached out and grabbed the metal. The silo stopped. The tower buckled in at the point where Clark was standing.

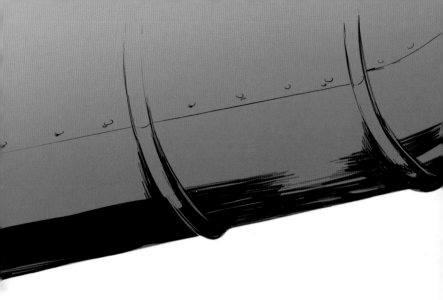

With a determined shove, Clark pushed the silo away from him. It rolled harmlessly across the cornfield.

Martha ran towards Clark and grabbed him. Jonathan joined them. Then all three hurried to the storm shelter and bolted the door behind them.

While the winds screamed above them, the family sat in the dim light of a small lamp. Martha never let go of Clark.

His arms stayed wrapped around her neck. Jonathan gazed at his newly adopted son.

"You did see what happened, didn't you, Martha?" he asked quietly.

Martha nodded, tears in her eyes. "We rescued Clark, and now he rescued us," she replied.

Jonathan took off his glasses and wiped them with a rag. "He's just a baby now," he said. "Think of what he could do when he grows up."

"We'll be good parents," said Martha softly. "We'll raise him as best we can."

Jonathan nodded. Then he reached over and patted the boy's shoulder. "You're a good boy, Clark," he said. "You did well, son."

The little hero looked up and smiled.

SUPERMAN

DC COMICS SUPER HEROES

THE MUSEUM MONSTERS

WRITTEN BY
MICHAEL DAHL

ILLUSTRATED BY
DAN SCHOENING

SUPERMAN CREATED BY
JERRY SIEGEL AND
JOE SHUSTER

BY SPECIAL
ARRANGEMENT WITH THE
JERRY SIEGEL FAMILY

CHAPTER 1

THE WORLD'S BIGGEST SKELETON

A flood of people swarmed outside the Metropolitan Museum of Natural History. They pushed against the glass and metal doors. They crowded the wide stone steps.

It was opening day. A new exhibit was on display: Monsters of the Deep. In half an hour the museum doors would open and thousands of visitors would rush inside.

At the back of the museum was a smaller door. It faced a quiet alley. There were no crowds back here. The museum director opened the door and peeked out.

"Quick!" he said. "Come in before anyone sees you!"

Two visitors followed him in. They were reporters for the *Daily Planet* newspaper, Lois Lane and Clark Kent. Lois threw her coat on a peg and rushed into the exhibit hall. Clark hurried to follow her.

"Thanks for letting us in early," said Lois Lane. "This will give us a chance to see the new exhibit before the crowd pours in."

"You probably want to see the biggest display first," said the museum director.

"By the way, have you seen our friend, Jimmy Olsen?" Clark asked. "He's supposed to come and take photos for our story."

The director frowned. "Sorry," he said. "I'm the only one here. Except for our security guards at the front doors."

"That's funny," said Clark. "Jimmy's always on time."

"Don't worry about him," said Lois. "He'll show up soon."

Clark heard a strange buzzing sound. He glanced around but saw nothing. At first he thought it was a fly zipping past his ear.

"Our biggest exhibit is right through here," said the director. He led Lois and Clark through a tall stone corridor. They entered a giant room that soared five stories above the marble floor.

In the centre of the room, hanging on metal wires high above their heads, was a huge skeleton.

"That's fantastic!" said Lois.

"It's the skeleton of a blue whale," explained the director. "The largest creature to ever live on the planet."

"Exactly how big is it?" asked Clark. He pulled out a small pad of paper and started jotting down notes.

The director stared up at the monster skeleton. "This one is over 33 metres long," he said. "When it was alive, it could hold over 80 tonnes of water in its mouth."

"Wow!" came a voice from nearby. "That whale's head is bigger than my whole apartment!"

"Jimmy!" said Lois.

At the other end of the large hall stood a redheaded teenager. He had a camera hanging from his neck and waved at the others. "Hi, Miss Lane. Hi, Mr Kent."

"Jimmy," said Clark. "How did you get in here?"

"I have my ways," said Jimmy, smiling.

Clark heard the buzzing sound again. No one else in the room seemed to notice it, but that was not unusual. Clark Kent was actually Superman in disguise, the world's most powerful hero. And one of Superman's powers was super-hearing. He could hear sounds from miles away.

What was that buzzing, he wondered.

The sound seemed to be coming from another room. Clark looked up at a sign above the room's door. ENTOMOLOGY. Clark knew that meant insects. Maybe the buzzing had come from an insect, just as he thought.

As the others continued staring at the whale skeleton, Clark quickly stepped inside the insect room. The buzzing grew louder. Now it didn't sound like an insect at all. It sounded like a tiny voice. In fact, his super-hearing could pick up words. The voice was saying, "Superman! Help me!"

CHAPTER 2

THE WORLD'S SMALLEST REPORTER

Clark glanced around the insect room. All he saw were glass cases that held insects from all over the world. The buzzing voice was coming from a case filled with leaves and branches. A sign on the case said:

WORLD'S SMALLEST REPORTER
Scientific Name: *J. Olsen*

Clark bent down to have a closer look. Inside the case sat a tiny, redheaded boy waving and screaming.

"Help me, Mr Kent!" the figure cried.

"Jimmy?" said Clark.

Quickly, Clark opened the lid of the case. He stuck in his hand and carefully picked up the tiny boy with his fingers. Then he set Jimmy on a nearby table. The boy stood no taller than the reporter's thumb.

"How did this happen?" asked Clark.

"I don't know," said Jimmy. "I was coming here to meet you and Miss Lane. The last thing I remember was knocking on the back door of the museum. Then I was inside that glass case. I could have ended up as insect food if you hadn't saved me."

Clark was confused. If this was the real Jimmy Olsen, who was the redheaded teenager in the other room? And who put the real Jimmy in the insect case?

Suddenly, a woman's scream echoed through the museum. AAAAAHHHHHHHHH!

"That's Lois," said Clark. "Will you be all right here, Jimmy?"

"No problem," said Jimmy. "I'll try to contact Superman with my signal-watch." Inside Jimmy's watch was a chip that could give off a supersonic beep. Only Superman's ears could hear the sound. "I hope it works at this size," added Jimmy.

"I think he's already here," said Clark.

"Really?" said Jimmy. While the teenager glanced around, searching for his superpowered friend, Clark raced out of the room. At the doorway to the whale exhibit, he froze. The blue whale's skeleton was moving. It swung back and forth.

At the other end of the room stood Lois and the museum director. Their eyes were glued to the moving skeleton.

"Watch out, Miss Lane!" warned the museum director.

TWANNNGG! One of the wires holding the skeleton snapped loose.

TWANNNGG! Another one broke.

Soon, the skeleton would crash to the floor. Clark dashed into a small nearby office. With super-speed he pulled off his reporter's clothes, revealing his Superman uniform underneath. Then he raced into the exhibit hall as the mighty Man of Steel.

"Superman!" yelled Lois.

He flew into the air. Another wire broke and the whale skeleton fell to the floor. Superman caught the skeleton easily in his arms. He gently set it on the shiny marble floor.

"Thank you, Superman!" the museum director cried. "That skeleton is priceless. If it had hit the floor, the bones would have shattered into a million pieces."

"Yes, thank you," added Lois.

Superman flew over to the reporter. "How did this happen?" he asked.

"I don't understand it," Lois said. "All of a sudden the skeleton began to shake."

Just then, the skeleton began to move its jaws. Its bony flippers waved up and down.

"It's alive!" said Lois.

"That's impossible!" said the museum director.

"It's very possible," said another voice. Superman turned to see Jimmy Olsen standing a few feet away.

The hero knew this was not the real Jimmy, but an impostor. The real Jimmy was still shrunk to tiny size in the insect room.

"Who are you?" asked the Man of Steel.

The fake Jimmy Olsen laughed. His face changed shape. His red hair disappeared. He grew shorter. Then he began to spin around faster and faster.

Suddenly, floating a few yards from Superman's face was a weird little man wearing a purple hat. "Who in the world is that?" asked Lois.

"That's just the problem," said Superman. "He's not from this world. It's Mr Mxyzptlk from the Fifth Dimension!"

CHAPTER 3

THE MISCHIEF MAKER

"Mr what?" asked Lois.

The odd little imp took off his hat and bowed. "Just call me Mxy," he said. "Only Super Duper Man has ever been able to pronounce my real name."

"What are you doing here?" demanded Superman.

"You don't sound very happy to see me," said Mr Mxyzptlk, frowning. "I came here to help you celebrate."

"Celebrate?" asked Superman.

"The opening of this amazing museum," said the strange imp. "Nobody knows how to have fun like me, isn't that right?"

The museum director was confused and annoyed. "You mean, it was you who caused those wires to break?" he yelled. "Do you have any idea of the damage you could have caused? These objects are priceless."

"You need to relax," said Mxy, pointing at the man. "Too much worrying can turn you into a bag of bones."

The museum director was changed into a living skeleton. His clothes hung on a frame of bones. His bony feet slipped out of his shoes. He was unable to speak because his tongue was gone.

"Turn him back," Superman ordered.

Mr Mxyzptlk ignored the super hero and flew towards the ceiling. "Let's have a party!" shouted the mischievous imp. He clapped his hands together.

"Now what's happening?" asked Lois.

A glittering whirlwind filled the room. Tiny lights of different colours sparkled and whirled around her and Superman. Soon, the lights grew larger and thicker. They looked like floating crystal bowls.

"Look out, Lois!" said Superman. "Those are flying jellyfish."

Hundreds of jellyfish swam through the air. Below their shining heads hung long spindly arms. These arms, or tentacles, each carried a poisonous stinger at the end. One stab of poison could kill a human.

Superman was not human. He was a visitor from the planet Krypton, which was light-years away from Earth. The Earth's yellow sun had given his alien body powers far beyond those of mortal men. But even he was helpless against the forces of Mr Mxyzptlk's magic. The stingers of these nightmare jellyfish might be able to stab even Superman's unbreakable skin.

"Don't you like my little friends?" said Mxy. "They're here to help us celebrate the wonderful world of sea creatures."

"Get behind me, Lois," said Superman.

The reporter ducked behind the man's massive shoulders. Then the super hero took in a deep breath. With the power of his superpowered lungs, he blew out a powerful wind. The wind shoved the jellyfish away from him and Lois.

"That's a great idea," said Mr Mxyzptlk with a laugh. "I always thought you were a blowhard. Now, you can be – a blowfish!"

Superman's body began to expand like a balloon. He stared in horror as his arms grew flat and flabby and then turned into flippers. His mouth grew wide. His uniform was covered with orange, prickly scales. Long spikes stuck out from his back, his sides, and his stomach.

The weird fish hung in the centre of the room. Its huge eyes stared in anger at the little imp. Meanwhile, Mxy was doubled over in laughter.

Lois Lane was so angry that tears came to her eyes. "You can't do that to Superman," she cried.

Mr Mxyzptlk stopped laughing. "Careful, Miss Lane," he said. "Otherwise Superfish might do something to you!"

Lois's eyes grew wide with fear. Just then, the giant blowfish made a gurgling noise. It sounded like a human voice trying to say, "Look out!"

Sharp, orange spikes shot from the fish's body. They flew in all directions throughout the room. One of the spikes, as large as a spear, flew past Lois's feet. She jumped and threw herself behind a stone display table for protection.

Another spike stabbed through the museum director's skeleton and pinned him to the wall. More spikes broke statues and chandeliers and displays.

"You're making a mess, Superman," said the little imp. He flew down from the ceiling and snapped his fingers. Superman returned to his normal size and shape.

"I think you look better like that," said Mxy. "But what are we going to do about all this clutter? Hmmm."

Superman flew to Lois's side.

"Superman, what will we do?" asked Lois. "His magic is too powerful even for you."

"There's only one way to defeat that imp," whispered the Man of Steel. "If he says his name backwards, then he's banished back to the Fifth Dimension."

"How do we get him to say it?" said Lois.

"I have an idea," said Superman. "But I'll need your help."

CHAPTER 4

OCEAN CREATURES

"Oh, Superman!" called the wicked imp.

Superman raced over to Mr Mxyzptlk. "Haven't you had enough fun, yet?" he asked the little man.

Mxy shook his head. "We have to clean up first," he said. "Didn't your mother ever tell you to pick up after you play?"

Lois looked over the edge of the stone table where she was hiding. What was Mxy planning next? Suddenly, her feet felt cold and wet.

Lois stared down at the marble floor. It was covered with an inch of warm water. "I have a bad feeling about this," she said.

Lois stood up and looked around the rest of the hall. Water was everywhere. The stairs to the second floor looked like a waterfall. In less than a minute, the water had reached her knees.

"Rub-a-dub-dub," said Mr Mxyzptlk. "Time to clean!"

Superman stood in the middle of the hall, water swirling around his boots. "This has gone far enough," he said.

Mxy zigged and zagged through the air. "Don't even think of getting rid of this water, Super Duper Man," he said. "Because our poor fishy friends couldn't live without it."

The level of the water was now up to Superman's chest. He flew over to Lois and lifted her up. "We're getting out of here now," he said.

"Not so fast," said the little imp. "I put a special jinx on your museum. You and Miss Lane can't leave the building. Besides, it would be very rude of you to leave before my celebration is over!"

Still held in Superman's arms, Lois asked, "What's that sound?"

Superman stared at the marble walls of the exhibit hall. His powerful X-ray vision let him see through the stone. He saw large glass tanks in another room break and fall apart. The tanks had been holding the museum's other famous residents. Sharks!

Two enormous hammerhead sharks swam down the steps and into the exhibit hall. Superman flew towards the ceiling. He set Lois down on a stone ledge high above the water. "Wait here," he told her. Then he zoomed into the insect room. He found Jimmy floating in the water, holding on to a wooden pencil.

"I knew you'd show up," said Jimmy.

Superman held Jimmy gently in his hand and then soared back to Lois. "I have something for you," said the Man of Steel.

Superman dropped the tiny boy in the woman's palm. "Don't tell me that's Jimmy!" she cried.

Jimmy held his hands to his ears. "Please, Miss Lane!" he said. "Not so loud."

"Hang on to the ledge," said Superman. "I've got to stop that imp somehow."

As he flew away, Lois called after him. "You have to find Clark Kent! He might be trapped in the museum!"

"I'll find him, Lois," said the super hero. "Don't worry."

The water rose higher and higher. More sea creatures were swimming below the sharks. Giant sea turtles and stingrays darted through the waves. Electric eels slithered and sparked.

The rushing water had been pressing against the windows of the museum. Now, several of the windows broke. The pressure was too strong. Water poured through the new openings like raging rivers, splashing on to the crowds outside.

"I'm not able to leave the museum to help those people," said Superman. "I can't break through Mxy's magic spell."

The Man of Steel flew back to the centre of the hall. He stared up at the ceiling. The wires that had held the whale skeleton were still dangling free. Superman tied them together with super-speed and made one long wire. Then he made a loop and swung it out a broken window.

Like a superpowered cowboy, he lassoed the sharks and turtles and pulled them back inside the building. Then he used his heat-vision to repair the window glass and weld them shut.

"It's not fair," said Mr Mxyzptlk. "I was trying to share my celebration with those silly people outside."

Then, the little imp snapped his fingers. "That's it!" he cried.

"Now what are you doing?" asked Superman. **RUMMMMMMMBLE!**

The Man of Steel stared out of a window. He couldn't believe his eyes. The museum was rising into the air. Mr Mxyzptlk had created gigantic crab legs on the bottom of the building. The stiff legs unfolded and lifted the entire museum off its foundation.

"The museum isn't a toy," Superman said. "You could seriously hurt someone."

"Don't be crabby," said Mxy. Then he chuckled. "Ha! I made a joke. Get it?"

Outside, men and women screamed. Taxis tried to rush away from the building but ran into other fleeing vehicles.

The huge museum monster began to march down the street. It scraped against other buildings on both sides of the street. Cement, metal, and broken glass rained down on the sidewalks.

"This show is going on the road," yelled Mxy happily. "If people can't visit the museum, then the museum will visit them. Isn't that a wonderful idea, Superman? Don't you think I'm generous?"

The little imp clapped his hands together and flew in a circle, round and round. Sparks flew out behind him like fireworks. "This is the best party ever!" he said. "And I'm the perfect host!"

CHAPTER 5

THE WORST MONSTER

The museum monster marched through Metropolis on its giant crab legs. Buildings were smashed. Cars were crushed. People were injured. Mr Mxyzptlk's selfish prank caused destruction throughout the city.

Superman stared out of the museum window, unable to help. He knew he had to do something.

Suddenly, he turned and faced the floating imp. "This is your most amazing trick ever," he said.

Mxy's face lit up with delight. "You think so?" he cried. "You really, really think so?"

Superman nodded. "Only someone as clever and thoughtful as you, Mxy, could come up with this celebration," he said. "The people of Metropolis will never forget you. They'll talk about your museum party for years to come."

Bright tears glistened in the imp's eyes. "Oh, I'm so happy," he said.

"It's perfect," said Superman. "Except for –" Then he stopped.

"Except for what?" asked Mr Mxyzptlk.

"Never mind," said Superman.

A worried frown covered the floating imp's face. "I want my party to be perfect," he wailed. "What else can I do, Superman?"

The Man of Steel stood for a moment in thought. "Well," he said slowly, "you want the people of Metropolis to enjoy the new exhibits at the museum, right?'

"Yes! Of course, I do," said Mr Mxyzptlk.

"I'm just a little worried that some of the exhibits may scare them," said Superman.

"Scare them? Which ones?" Mxy asked.

Superman pointed up the marble stairs toward the upper floors. "We have an exhibit of dangerous animals," he said. "One of them is the creature that's most frightening to humans."

Mxy's eyes grew wide under his purple hat. "Really?" he asked in a whisper. "What is it called?"

"Humans don't even like the sound of its name," said Superman.

Superman leaned in closer. "Parents use the name to frighten bad children," he said. "But even grown-ups hate to hear it."

Mr Mxyzptlk clapped his hands together. "I must see it," he cried. "If it is the world's worst monster, I must learn all about it. It would make a perfect pet!"

"Please, Mxy," said Superman in a serious tone. "Don't force people to see it. As I said, humans are terrified of the creature."

Mr Mxyzptlk had an evil grin. "Oh, don't worry," he said. "I'll be very careful. You know how kind and caring I am."

Superman stared at the imp. "Very well," he said. "I'll show you the monster. Follow me." The Man of Steel flew up the marble stairs with the little man close behind him.

They soon arrived at another exhibit hall on the fourth floor. In the centre of the room stood a tall, hairy stuffed animal. It had the body of a bear, the tusks of an elephant, the mane of a lion, and the long snout of an alligator. A long anteater's tongue dripped out of its jaws.

"It looks horrible." said Mr Mxyzptlk.

"I told you," said Superman. "Now remember, don't even say the creature's name when you're around people. Humans hate the sound of it."

The little imp chuckled to himself. "They do, do they? Why, I'd never want to frighten people. Hmmmm."

Mr Mxyzptlk moved closer to the terrible creature. He bent down and read the name of the creature on a metal sign.

Then Mr Mxyzptlk read the sign aloud:

THE WORLD'S WORST MONSTER
Scientific Name: *Kltp Zyxm*

"Superman! You tricked me!" screamed the little imp. "You made me say my name backwards!"

Superman crossed his arms and smiled. "Goodbye, Mxy. Enjoy the Fifth Dimension."

The little man began to fade. His purple hat and tiny boots were just dark smudges on the air. "There is no creature like that, is there, Superman?" he asked.

"Of course, not, Mxy. I made it up," said the Man of Steel. "I used parts of different animals on display throughout the museum. With my super-speed, I took the parts and made this fake animal. I moved so fast you never even saw me do it."

THE WORLD'S
WORST MONSTER

SCIENTIFIC NAME: KLTP ZYXM

"AAAAAAAAhhhhhhhhhhh!" With a loud **POP!** the little imp disappeared.

Superman flew downstairs to rescue Lois and Jimmy from the ledge near the ceiling. As he did, a strange thing happened. The museum's crab legs vanished. The whale skeleton was hanging back on its wires. Jimmy was his regular size. The museum director was no longer just a walking skeleton. The crowds outside acted like nothing had happened that morning.

"Is it all over?" asked Lois.

"When Mr Mxyzptlk returned to his home dimension, all his magic disappeared with him," said Superman.

Jimmy Olsen gazed out a window. "Wow," he said. "The museum is back in its regular place. It's like it never even moved."

The museum director rushed up to Superman and shook his hand. "Thank you, Superman. I owe you my life," he said. "And if you'll please excuse me," he added, looking at his watch, "I need to let in our visitors."

He raced away to the front doors.

Suddenly, Lois looked worried. "I forgot about Clark," she said. "He was somewhere in the building. Oh, Jimmy, you don't think he drowned, do you?"

"Don't worry, Lois," said Superman. "He's just fine. I saw him rush outside looking for the police earlier. Luckily, he never got trapped inside with the rest of us."

"But now he's caught in that crowd," said Jimmy. "Poor Mr Kent."

Lois simply shook her head. "Clark Kent always seems to miss the action," she said. Then she turned to look at the Man of Steel. "It's a good thing you never do, Superman."

But the super hero had already flown away.

SUPERMAN

TOYS OF TERROR

WRITTEN BY
CHRIS EVERHEART

ILLUSTRATED BY
JOHN DELANEY AND
LEE LOUGHRIDGE

SUPERMAN CREATED BY
JERRY SIEGEL AND
JOE SHUSTER

BY SPECIAL
ARRANGEMENT WITH THE
JERRY SIEGEL FAMILY

CHAPTER 1

SURPRISE PACKAGES

The Christmas float pulled to a stop outside a toy shop in central Metropolis. A crowd of little kids cheered. Reporters Clark Kent and Lois Lane made their way through the smiling faces. They were here to write a story for their newspaper, the *Daily Planet*.

"This is the biggest crowd I've ever seen for the Christmas parade," said Lois.

"The ad on TV said there would be free toys," Clark said. "That always attracts a crowd."

The two reporters stopped near the float. A huge Christmas tree stood in the middle of the float. It sparkled with colourful twinkling lights. A pile of brightly wrapped presents sat under it.

The children cheered, looking for the jolly old man with a white beard. Instead a big, beefy man stepped on to the float. He wore a red Santa suit. His boots and belt were as black as his hair. He had mean eyes and a scar on his right cheek.

The crowd went silent. Some of the children frowned. A few of them turned away.

"Clark, isn't that –?" Lois began to ask.

Clark gave a quick nod. "Bruno 'Ugly' Mannheim," he said.

"Wasn't he in jail?" Lois asked.

"He was in jail," said Clark. "Superman caught him robbing a bank last year."

"Then what's he doing on that float?" asked Lois.

Clark watched Bruno closely. "Maybe he's here to steal Christmas," he joked.

Just then Bruno Mannheim spoke up. "Hello, children," he said. "I am so happy to see all of you! You see, I've just got out of jail. I learned a lot while paying for my crimes. I have been a bad, bad man. But starting today, I'm going to change." Bruno looked over at Clark and Lois.

"So that's his game," said Clark. "He wants us to think he's a good guy now."

Bruno raised his hands and continued, "Children of Metropolis, these are my gifts to you!"

Bruno reached under the tree and grabbed an armful of presents. He started throwing colourful boxes into the crowd. The children cheered.

"The kids certainly think he's a good guy now!" said Lois.

As the parade float neared the reporters, Bruno looked down at Lois. "Miss Lane, would you join me on the float?" he asked politely, holding out his hand. "You've been my toughest critic. I want to show you exactly how much I've changed."

Lois smiled and took a step toward the float. Clark Kent quickly grabbed her arm. "Be careful, Lois," he warned. "I have a funny feeling about this."

Lois smiled. "What's the matter?" she asked. "Jealous that I'm getting the scoop?"

Lois grabbed Bruno's hand and stepped on to the float. Wrapping paper was flying everywhere. The children shouted with joy as they saw their presents.

"You see, Miss Lane?" Bruno said, looking out at the crowd. "I've learned my lesson. I'm all about spreading joy and happiness."

Lois pointed towards the back of the float. A group of tough-looking men stood on the street, frowning. "If you're such a good guy, Bruno, why are those thugs still hanging around? They don't look joyful or happy to me," she said.

"Them?" said Bruno, smiling. "They're my bodyguards."

"You can fool children with a few gifts," said Lois. "But you can't fool me."

Bruno's mouth turned up in a crooked grin. "That hurts, Miss Lane," he said. Then he waved to some kids in the crowd. "Come up on the float, kids! Show everyone your presents."

Five kids jumped on the float. One boy waved his box. "It's a helicopter!" he shouted. "Cool!"

Bruno scowled. "A helicopter?" he asked, slightly puzzled.

A little girl held an open box over her head. "I got a helicopter, too!" she exclaimed.

All of the children opened boxes to discover the same toy.

"Those were supposed to be dolls and toy soldiers!" Bruno muttered. "What's going on?"

Suddenly, a girl screamed. Her little helicopter zoomed out of its box and flew around her head. Then all the other boxes burst apart. Every helicopter started flying.

The choppers circled the crowd. They buzzed just above the kids' heads. The tiny cannons on the toys squirted a sticky, yellow-orange liquid. The children screamed and started to run.

CHAPTER 2

RUNAWAY FLOAT

The little helicopters swarmed towards the float. Lois ducked the whirling blades.

"So this was your plan, Bruno?" she shouted. "This is bad even for you!"

Bruno waved off an attacking helicopter. "This wasn't supposed to happen!" he said. "I stole a load of dolls and toy soldiers from a warehouse! Someone switched them for these nasty choppers!"

Clark Kent called from the street, "Lois, look out!"

A group of helicopters circled in the air above the kids and their parents. Any second now, it looked like they were going to shoot more sticky liquid from their guns.

Near the float, Bruno's men were also dodging the helicopters. One crook pulled out a huge pistol and started shooting into the air, aiming to hit a helicopter.

BANG! He missed. The choppers attacked the thugs like a flock of angry metal birds. The men yelled and jumped into a nearby car for safety.

Clark looked around to make sure no one was watching him. Then he inhaled and blew out a huge super-breath. The circling helicopters went spinning away on the wind. Clark kept blowing until the dangerous toys were blown far down the street.

"The helicopters are flying away!" a kid yelled.

"Let's get out of here!" shouted another.

Then Clark heard tyres screeching. He looked over to see Bruno's Christmas float jump forward and speed away. Clark knew this was serious trouble. He started looking for a place to slip away and change into his Superman uniform.

The car carrying Bruno's thugs tore off after the float. They didn't want to let their boss get away without them.

On the float, Lois and the kids screamed. Bruno grabbed hold of the Christmas tree. He fell backwards, tearing off a branch. Presents flew off the float and scattered into the street.

"Who's driving the float?" yelled Lois.

"I don't know," Bruno answered.

Lois tried to gather the kids. "Lay down flat," she told them. "Hold on tight!"

Bruno was frightened. He shouted below to where the driver sat, "Stop this thing! Now!"

"You won't get away with kidnapping me and these children, Bruno!" shouted Lois.

"I'm not doing this!" Bruno cried.

The float raced down the street. It took a sharp turn around a corner.

SKREEE-EEE-EEECH!

Lois was thrown sideways and rolled across the deck of the float. To her surprise, she found herself staring into a small window in front of the driver.

Even though Lois was bundled up against the cold, a deep shiver went down her back. She realized now that Bruno Mannheim was telling the truth. The out-of-control float was not his idea. Lois could see into the driver's seat. She saw an evil smile, staring eyes, and a little bow tie. The crazy driver was not one of Bruno's men. It was Bruno's enemy.

The Toyman!

CHAPTER 3

THE TOYMAN

The Toyman always wore a mask with a horrible grin, but at this moment he sounded angry. "Move aside, Miss Lane!" he shouted. "I can't see where I'm going! Do you want me to have an accident?"

"Toyman!" shouted Lois. "I should have known!"

"But you didn't," the Toyman snapped. "My plan was perfect. And it's working."

"Attacking children with helicopters?" Lois said. "You should be ashamed!"

The float swerved as the Toyman jerked the wheel to the right. Lois held on tight.

"Bruno's the one who should be ashamed," the Toyman shouted. "He thinks he can clean up his image by giving away a few toys? Hah! I'll show him!"

Bruno crawled over to the window beside Lois Lane. His face was red with anger. "Toyman, you'll be sorry for this," he said.

The Toyman laughed. "You're the one who's going to be sorry," he said. "You'll wish that you'd never killed my father!"

"I didn't kill your father," Bruno said. "He killed himself!"

"Because you ruined his business!" shouted Toyman. "Now you'll finally pay!" He turned the steering wheel sharply. Bruno and Lois rolled away from the window.

The Toyman looked in his rearview mirror. He saw the black car filled with Bruno's men. They were close behind and catching up to the float.

"Here are some toys for your boys to play with," the Toyman sneered.

He pulled a lever next to the seat. A hatch opened under the float's rear bumper. Ten little windup robots dropped on to the street. They wandered around in circles, cranking and buzzing. When the black car reached them, the robots started exploding.

In the car, one of the thugs yelled, "Look out!" The driver swerved around the bursting robots. But the explosion rocked the car. The windows were blown out.

"Bruno must be crazy!" one of the men shouted. "Why is he trying to stop us?"

Toyman looked at the street ahead. There, standing in the middle of the road was a tall figure in red and blue. Superman!

"Drat his super-speed!" Toyman said to himself. "Those helicopters should have kept him busy longer."

Superman watched the float race towards him and the black car following behind. Using his X-ray vision, Superman searched the inside of the float. There, in the driver's seat, he recognized the Toyman. The children and Lois were in danger!

The Toyman pushed a button on the dashboard. "Good thing I planned for this," he said.

Superman saw a small door open on the front of the float. "What's he up to now?" Superman wondered.

A blast shot out of the little door like a machine gun. Superman saw a flock of yellow rubber duckies coming at him. They looked so cute and harmless. But Superman knew Toyman better. He wasn't surprised when the first ducky began to swell up like a giant balloon.

All of the duckies began to grow larger. Their rubbery sides stuck together. Soon, they had turned into a huge yellow barrier surrounding the Man of Steel. Then they puffed up even more. Superman was trapped inside a gigantic ball of rubber.

"Nice try, Toyman," said Superman.

The hero began to spin. The yellow ducky balloons span around with him. Faster and faster he whirled. The yellow rubber moved so quickly that it began to burn up. Soon, it had sizzled away. Bits of burning rubber duckies littered the street.

"Superman! Help!" cried Lois from the speeding float.

The kids' eyes were wide with fear. "Superman!" they screamed.

Superman decided he could catch up to the float in a minute. First he would take care of Bruno's thugs. He jumped back into the road. He set his feet down on the street and reached forward. The black car sped towards him. When the men inside saw the super hero, they all shouted at once. The tyres skidded and screeched, but it was too late.

The car slammed right into the Man of Steel. The front end folded up as if it hit a telephone pole. Superman skidded backwards as the car ground to a stop. The radiator smoked. The engine coughed and spluttered.

The thugs looked up at Superman, shocked and amazed.

"Sorry boys," Superman said. "I can't risk you running into someone while I'm trying to save your boss. I'll take care of Bruno and the Toyman."

"Toyman?" muttered one of the crooks. "Is he behind all this?"

Superman shot up into the air and out of sight.

CHAPTER 4

THE TOY FACTORY OF TERROR

The Toyman chuckled when he knew Superman was no longer in sight. He drove the float into a tunnel and descended below the city streets. The kids were scared in the dark. They huddled close to Lois.

"Where are we going?" Lois shouted.

"Yeah," said Bruno, "where do you think you're taking us?"

The Toyman didn't answer. Instead, he stopped the float in the middle of the tunnel. Steel doors opened in front of them.

Meanwhile, in the sky above Metropolis, Superman flew in search of the Toyman's float. He used his super-vision to magnify the streets below. He followed the route where Toyman and the float should have gone. But they were missing. Where could they be?

Underground, the float rolled through the steel doors. Inside was an old factory, piled high with broken toy parts. Dolls' heads and toy soldiers' arms were heaped on the floor. A thousand jack-in-the-boxes without the jacks leaned against the walls.

When the float finally stopped, Lois, Bruno, and the children got off. The strange scene scared the kids more than the dark tunnel. Some began to cry.

"Don't worry," said Lois. "Superman will find us. This will all be over soon."

The Toyman emerged from the float and looked down at his prisoners. His eyes were cruel and cold above his wide smile. "Yes. Don't worry, kids. Bruno will be finished soon," he told them.

"Let the kids go, Toyman," said Lois. "They didn't do anything to you."

"I don't care about them," the Toyman said. "I'm after Bruno. He owes me big-time. And nothing will stop me."

Bruno Mannheim stood up. "Take the kids, Toyman," he said. "You can ransom them back to their parents. You'll make a fortune. Just let me go."

Lois turned to the crook who was still dressed in his Santa outfit. "These are innocent kids," she said. Be a man and face the Toyman yourself!"

Bruno waved a hand. "Ah, Toyman won't hurt them. Especially since they're worth so much money."

CLINK CLINK CLINK

Lois turned to see the Toyman walking up a set of steel stairs. The mask with its weird grin was still stuck on his face.

"It's too bad these kids trusted Bruno," the Toyman said. "If they're foolish enough to trust this crook, they deserve what they get."

Soon the Toyman had reached a platform high above the factory floor. He pulled a remote control out of his pocket. "I've built a special toy for you, Bruno," he said. "I think your new young friends will enjoy it." Toyman pushed a button on the remote control.

Lois heard a bounce and a squeak. The noise grew louder. The kids pushed themselves closer. She hugged them tightly.

BOUNCE! SQUEAK! A football bounced out from behind a pile of toy cars. It stopped in the middle of the floor.

Everyone relaxed. Lois sighed, and Bruno smiled.

"What's that supposed to be?" Bruno laughed. "You're going to kill me with a football?"

"It's so much more than a football," said the Toyman from his perch. He pushed another button on the remote. "Let's play," he said.

ZZRRRRTT! ZZRRRRTT! The football started to vibrate. Everyone closed their eyes, expecting it to blow up.

But instead of exploding, it opened with a **SNAP!** A dozen blades, sharp as razors, poked out of the ball. The ball started rolling across the floor. The squeak was gone. The sharp blades scraped as they moved against the concrete.

The children screamed.

The football rolled towards them. Lois grabbed the kids. She pulled them away from the deadly ball.

"Toyman, don't do this!" shouted Lois. She looked up at his perch. The little villain's evil mask glowed with happiness.

"I've finally got Bruno Mannheim right where I want him," the Toyman said. "I have him trapped, and Superman can't get in my way. It's brilliant. Don't you think, Miss Lane?"

Lois was scared. "Turn Bruno over to the police," she pleaded. "Let them take care of him."

"My super football is much more efficient, Miss Lane," Toyman said. He jumped back on to the floor and laughed. "And when it's done, there won't be anything left to find."

Lois looked over and saw Bruno climbing the Christmas tree on the float. "Get back here, you coward!" she shouted.

Bruno looked down at her and the kids. "Forget it. You're on your own," he called.

The football turned towards Lois and the children. It chased them into a corner. The knives were flashing and slicing through the air.

CHAPTER 5

TRAPPED!

"My life's work is almost done," the Toyman said. "I'll finally avenge my father's death."

"But these kids have fathers, too," said Lois, still huddling close to the children on the floor.

"Boo hoo," said the Toyman with a laugh.

"Hurry, children," shouted Lois. She pulled them back on to the float. "I think we'll be safe up here."

"Oh no!" shouted one of the kids.

A thin metal arm reached out of the football. It grabbed the side of the float and pulled itself up. The football started climbing on to the float. It was getting closer to the kids. They started to back away but couldn't go any further.

"Quick," said Lois. "Jump!"

The children jumped to the floor. Just then, the blades on the ball span like circular saws. They cut a path through the float like a soft stick of butter.

All eyes turned to the ceiling. A ray of sunlight poured through a hole. Then suddenly, the children saw a different ray of hope.

"Superman!" the children shouted.

In a second, Superman was on the float. He kicked the soccer ball away. The toy and its blades bounced against the factory wall.

"Blast you, Superman!" shouted the Toyman.

The Toyman pushed another button on his remote control. At his command, the football bounced off the wall and came flying back. This time it was spinning a hundred times faster than before.

"You won't ruin my revenge, Superman!" shouted the Toyman. "I'll cut you to super ribbons!"

Lois pointed and shouted, "Superman, look out!"

Superman turned and saw the football. It cut through the air at lightning speed. Superman span on one foot and threw a back kick. The ball bounced off his heel and flew towards the Toyman.

The little villain punched frantically at more buttons on his remote control. It was too late.

The bladed football spun upwards and then crashed down in front of him. Sparks flew off the metal. Then the ball flew past the Toyman, shredding his bow tie.

"Aaaahhhhhh!" Toyman screamed.

The ball smashed into the ceiling above his head and broke into pieces.

The Toyman ducked, trying to avoid the falling metal blades. His tiny shoe slipped on the floor. He fell backwards and landed in a pile of empty jack-in-the-boxes.

"No!" he cried.

Hundreds of boxes tumbled down, trapping the Toyman beneath their combined weight.

As the boxes moved, their handles turned. The factory was filled with the happy sounds of "Pop Goes the Weasel."

"I don't think this little weasel is going to pop up anytime soon," said Superman.

He turned to Lois and the children. "Don't worry, kids," he said. "You'll be back with your parents soon."

"Are you all right, Miss Lane?" Superman asked.

Just then, Bruno Mannheim climbed down from the top of the Christmas tree. "Whoa, that was close," he said. "What took you so long?"

Superman grinned. Then he looked at the dark factory. "The walls of Toyman's hideout are made of lead. I wasn't able to use my X-ray vision to find you.

"That slowed me down a little," Superman continued. "But then, thanks to Miss Lane's clues, I soon followed you here."

Bruno and the kids stared at her. "Her clues?" asked the crook.

"Yes," said Superman. "Miss Lane dropped her shoes along the road. Then she dropped her notepad. I followed the direction of the clues, and it led me straight to this abandoned building."

Lois looked down at her bare feet. Her shoes must have fallen off when the Toyman swerved the float back and forth along the road. In all the excitement, she hadn't even noticed they were gone.

"Quick thinking, Miss Lane," said Superman.

"Uh, thanks," she said.

Bruno held his hand out to the super hero. "Well, thanks loads, Superman," he said. "It's nice to be working together for a change. See you later."

"I've got someone coming to pick you up, Bruno," said Superman.

Bruno smiled. "My boys?" he asked, hopefully.

"No, *my* boys," Superman smiled.

A police siren sounded in the distance.

"Hey, wait a minute!" shouted Bruno. "The Toyman was after me. He was trying to kill me. I'm the victim here."

"And what about all those stolen presents you were going to hand out at the parade?" asked Superman.

Bruno frowned. "Oh, right." He looked at the broken dolls and soldiers that littered the Toyman's factory. The little villain had replaced them with his helicopters in the warehouse that Bruno had broken into earlier.

Lois stepped up to Superman. "I don't know how to thank you, Superman," she said. "You're always nearby when I –" She noticed the kids staring up at the Man of Steel. "I mean, when we need you."

"I wish I could stay, Miss Lane," he said, "but there's more crime to fight in Metropolis. The holidays are always a busy time."

"I can't wait to get back to the *Daily Planet* and write this story," said Lois. "Poor Clark is missing out on the whole thing."

Superman smiled. "Oh, I get the feeling Clark is nearby," he said.

The Man of Steel waved at the kids. He then grabbed Toyman and shot up through the hole in the roof. He became a red and blue streak, then disappeared.

"Well, kids," said Lois, staring up at the empty sky. "Merry Christmas."